THE Yin-Yang Sisters AND THE Dragon Frightful

Nancy Tupper Ling

illustrated by
Andrea Offermann

G. P. PUTNAM'S SONS

The villagers of Woo lived in fear of the dragon Frightful. His shadow wrapped around their town. His claws dug into their land, and when he snored, their houses shook like grains of rice.

Just when it seemed things couldn't get any worse, they did.

One hot summer day,
Frightful stretched his
scaly body all the way
across the Dan-Tat Bridge,
and there he stayed.

To reach the market, the villagers now had to trudge over two high hills and across another long bridge.

On that very day, the Lee twins were born. Baba and Mama were doubly happy. So was Mama's sister, YiYi.

When their
wise auntie
peered into their
crib, baby Wei
opened her eyes
and raised her
fist. Baby Mei
closed her eyes
and sucked
her thumb.

"Just like yin and yang. Two are stronger than one," YiYi said. "Together you'll grow to fight that dragon."

Years went by, and no one could
frighten that dragon away, until . . .

"I'll scare him," Wei said when she turned five. She liked to swing from tall trees and fly her kite on the very top of Hunan Mountain.

"Not me." Mei shook her head. She liked to wrap dumplings and fold paper lilies.

After dinner, Wei looked around at her family. They were so tired from climbing the two high hills and crossing the long bridge every day.

"That dragon won't stop us anymore!" Wei cried. Then she stomped out the door.

Mei felt oozy all over.

Frightful could singe them
with one fiery puff.

Still, they were sisters.

They stuck together.

"Let me pass," Wei shouted at Frightful. Then she stuck out her tongue.

Frightful took one long steamy breath, ready to blow Wei back home.

"Look, look!" Mei pointed
at the evening clouds. "A
spotted-dotted phoenix!"

When Frightful
looked up, Mei pulled
her sister away.
"*Please*," Mei begged.
"Don't do that again!"
Wei hugged her sister.
"You saved me," she said.

And things in the
village went back to
normal. But how the
villagers still wished for
someone to frighten
that dragon!

On their next birthday, YiYi said, "Like the Harvest and Budding Moons, together they'll scare that dragon away."

"Yes, yes!" said Wei. She began to think of a plan.

"Not me," said Mei. "He's far too frightful."

That night, Mei dreamed that Frightful set their town on fire. When she woke, she had an idea.

Mei worked all day at
Master Long's metal shop.

When she was done, she smiled.
Her invention was perfect for someone
brave like Wei.

Just then, Wei ran past the door.

"Wait, wait!" Mei called. "Take this!"
But she was too late.

Wei was headed toward the
Dan-Tat Bridge.

Mei felt oozy all over.

Still, they were sisters.

They stuck together.

Frightful stood between the twins
and poor Baba. The dragon was big
and stinky; he could swallow them
with one gulp.

"Let him pass, dragon," Wei said,
throwing a handful of hot peppers
right into Frightful's nose.

"Ah . . . ahhh . . ." Frightful sniffed.

Mei grabbed her sister's
hand. "Quick—jump under
here!" she said.

"CHOOOOOOOOOOOOOOOOOOOOOO!"

Frightful sneezed.

"*Please,*" Mei said.
"Don't do that anymore."
   Wei hugged her sister.
"You saved me again,"
she said.
   The villagers were
talking now. Could the
sisters really frighten
that dragon?

On their next birthday, YiYi said, "Like the bamboo and the birch tree, together they'll scare that dragon away."

"Of course," said Wei as she ran to her kung fu lessons.

"Not me!" said Mei. She
headed to Madam Liu's library.
"Hmm," Mei said. "I never
knew *that*. This could help
someone brave like Wei."

The next
morning,
the sisters
climbed
the two
high hills
and crossed
the long
bridge to the
market.

And they crossed the long bridge and climbed the two high hills to get home. They were exhausted.

Then Wei saw Frightful.

She headed right to him and—
POW!—she flip-flopped that dragon
with her best kung fu.

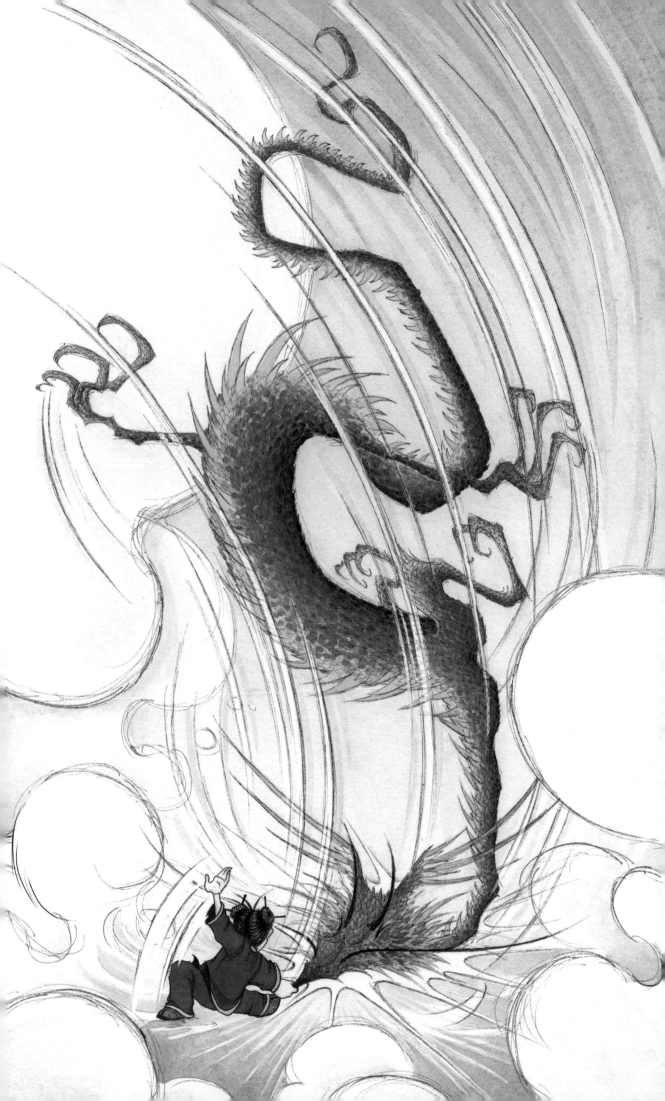

Frightful wrapped his tail around
Wei and swung her high into the air.
The whole village stared in silence.
No one moved.

Mei knew she was going to have
to do something very brave. And so
she swallowed her oozy feeling.

"Put her down, dragon!"
Mei said. No one heard her.

"Put her down!"
she tried again. Frightful
didn't even blink. Mei
took a deep breath.

"PUT HER DOWN
AND LET US PASS!"
she shouted.

"No way!" said Frightful.

"WHY NOT?" shouted Mei.

Frightful paused. He'd never been asked *that* question before. "Because . . . because I'm a scary dragon, that's why."

"Everyone knows dragons are sweet," Mei said. "See, it says so right here. All you need is a sticky bun now and then."

"I do?" Frightful asked.

"Of course," Mei replied.

With that, she pulled
five of Chef Wu's famous
buns out of her pocket.
Frightful licked the buns
right out of her hand.

Then that
dragon smiled
the happiest,
stickiest smile
the villagers had
ever seen, and
he let everyone
pass over the
Dan-Tat Bridge.

"You did it!" the villagers cried.
"You made our dragon happy."
Mei and Wei smiled.

"With a little yin," said Wei.

"And a little yang," said Mei.

"Together we make the perfect pair."

And to this day, the villagers bring
treats to that sticky bun dragon,
for Frightful is now most
Delightful.